129020

Hayner Public Library District - Alton

0 00 30 0447176 3

D1369994

HAYNER PUBLIC LIBRARY DISTRICT
ALTON, ILLINOIS

OVERDUES .10 PER DAY MAXIMUM FINE
COST OF BOOKS. LOST OR DAMAGED
BOOKS ADDITIONAL $5.00 SERVICE CHARGE.

UNDER THE
MISHMASH TREES

DiCK KiNG-SMiTH
UNDER THE MISHMASH TREES

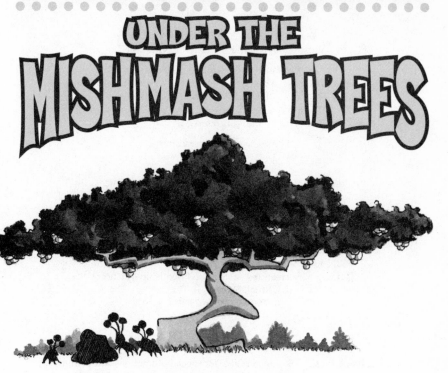

ILLUSTRATED BY
NiCK BRUEL

Roaring Brook Press
New York

HAYNER PUBLIC LIBRARY DISTRICT
ALTON, ILLINOIS

Text copyright © 2005 by Foxbusters Ltd.
Illustrations copyright © 2008 by Nick Bruel

Published by Roaring Brook Press
Roaring Brook Press is a division of Holtzbrinck Publishing Holdings
Limited Partnership
175 Fifth Avenue, New York, New York 10010
All rights reserved

Book design by Jaime Putorti

Library of Congress Cataloging-in-Publication Data
King-Smith, Dick.
Under the mishmash trees / Dick King-Smith ; illustrated by Nick Bruel.—1st
American ed.   p. cm.
Summary: Tells the story of an unlikely friendship that develops among Og and Ut,
who are gombrizils, and Tumblerum Wollycobble, a slobbadunk.
ISBN-13: 978-1-59643-325-0   ISBN-10: 1-59643-325-6
[1. Imaginary creatures—Fiction. 2. Friendship—Fiction.]
I. Bruel, Nick, ill. II. Title.
PZ7.K5893Un 2008
[Fic]—dc22
2007023919

Roaring Brook Press books are available for special promotions and premiums.
For details contact: Director of Special Markets, Holtzbrinck Publishers.

First published in Great Britain by Puffin Books, an imprint of the Penguin Group

Printed in the United States of America
First American Edition May 2008
1 3 5 7 9 10 8 6 4 2

E
KIN

618121585

For my good friend Richard Lavalliere
—N.B.

"If there's one creature I can't stand," said Og, "it's a slobbadunk."

Og was a gombrizil. All gombrizils have very short names and very long legs. Slobbadunks, on the other hand, have very long names and no legs at all.

Generally speaking, gombrizils get along quite well with slobbadunks, but Og was the exception.

"I can't stick 'em," he said to Ut, his wife, as they stood side by side under the mishmash trees. "They make me feel physically sick."

"I know, dear," said Ut. "Perhaps you were frightened by one when you were very small. None of the rest of us mind them, they're harmless. Look, here's one coming along now, it won't hurt you."

"Ugh!" cried Og. "Horrible thing! Hold my leg, Ut, I'm scared!"

Ut wrapped two of her seven long legs around one of Og's as the slobbadunk approached very slowly, sliding along on its huge stomach. It was staring at Og with the one large green eye in the middle of its forehead. It opened its round rubbery mouth and burped. Og began to cry.

"Go away!" shouted Ut to the slobbadunk. "You are frightening my husband."

The slobbadunk slithered to a halt.

"Sorry," it said in a very deep voice. It burped again. "Must be something I ate," it said. "I'm a martyr to indigestion. It runs in the family: We all suffer from gas, all us Wollycobbles. By the way, allow me to introduce myself. My name is Tumblerum Wollycobble."

"Are you a boy or a girl?" asked Ut.

"Both, madam," said the slobbadunk. "Most of us are."

It spoke so politely to the two gombrizils that Ut felt she should tell it her name in return; so she did.

"Ut what?" asked Tumblerum Wollycobble.

"Just Ut."

"Oh. And your husband's name?"

"Og."

"Og what?"

"Just Og."

"Why is he crying, madam?" asked the slobbadunk.

"He's scared of you," said Ut.

"But we're quite harmless."

"Yes, I know," said Ut, "but the fact remains that Og can't stand slobbadunks."

"Oh," said Tumblerum Wollycobble.

There was a hurt look in its green eye, Ut could see, and once again it opened its round rubbery mouth as if to say something more, but all that came out was another belch. Then it slithered away, rather sadly, Ut thought.

But Og, seeing it depart, became brave and started shouting rude things after it, like "Windbag!" and "Smellybreath!"

Ut unwrapped the two legs with which she had been holding her husband.

"I'll tell you something, Og," she said. "You are not a very nice gombrizil. I've a good mind to divorce you."

"Feel free," said Og. "I can soon find another wife."

Ut stood up very tall on her seven long legs, staring angrily at Og out of her three stalky eyes. Female gombrizils are quite a bit bigger than the males, and, for a moment, it looked as though Og might live to regret his words. But just then a noisy flock of strollops flew into the nearby mishmash trees.

Strollops are great carriers of news, especially bad news. Looking down in flight, they see everything that is going on below, and they tell the world about it in their shrill voices. Seldom can any creature do anything without the strollops knowing, and even a minor accident is loudly reported.

Now they perched in the tops of the mishmash trees, screeching loudly, but Ut and Og were too angry with each other to listen to their message.

"Trouble!" squawked the strollops. "The slobbadunk's in trouble!"

Ut turned away and flounced off in the direction that Tumblerum Wollycobble had taken, and Og went off the opposite way, sulkily.

Ut made her way through the trees, moving jerkily as all gombrizils do. Six of their seven legs stick out, three on each side, rather like the oars of a rowboat. The seventh, which is the largest, grows beneath their chins.

With this seventh leg Ut reached out, planting

the claw on its end firmly into the
ground ahead, to pull herself
forward. At the same time,
she sculled with all the
other six legs together,
which resulted in a kind
of huge hop.

No one can say that
gombrizils are graceful, but
they can move remarkably
quickly if necessary, as when pursuing various
small creatures on which they feed, such as spuddicks, swoots, or filigogs.

Ut was in fact not hungry at this moment,
but angry—with herself. *Silly me,* she thought
as she hopped along, *talking about divorce like
that; the last thing I want really. I don't want to
lose Og, he's so handsome. I just wish he wasn't so
beastly to slobbadunks. Not only is he nasty to them,*

*he's frightened of them, too, silly
boy.*

Just then Ut heard, not far
ahead, a sudden loud deep
voice.

"Help!" it called. "Help
me, please, someone!"

That's Tumblerum Wollycobble, she thought,
and she hopped her fastest until she came to a
meadow of slippysloppy grass, in the middle of
which lay the fat figure of the slobbadunk. As it
heard Ut approaching, its round rubbery mouth
opened.

"I don't know who you are," it said, "but could
you help me?"

"I'm Ut," said Ut, "the gombrizil. Don't you
remember me?"

"Oh, madam!" cried the slobbadunk. "Of
course I remember you. How could I ever

forget you? But I shall never again see your kind face."

"Why not?" asked Ut.

"Because, madam," said Tumblerum Wollycobble, "I have been struck blind! It happened so suddenly. One minute I could see as clearly as usual, the next I could see nothing! Alas, I have lost the use of my eye, my only eye."

Ut drew closer and looked carefully at the middle of the slobbadunk's forehead. There was indeed no sign of that one green eye, and Ut could now see why. The field of slippysloppy grass was a very wet one and somehow, a lump of mud, thrown up perhaps by an extra large belch as the slobbadunk grazed, had landed on its eye and blanked out its sight.

But before Ut could say anything, a torrent of words burst from Tumblerum Wollycobble's round rubbery mouth.

"Oh, madam!" it cried. "What a sorry slob-badunk am I! Never again shall I see your kindly face or that of your noble husband. Never again shall I see the happy hopping of the bushy-tailed filigogs, nor the long ears of the spuddicks, nor the soft shells of the hagafists. Never again shall I see the strollops flying up to perch and preen and pick the freeble fruits from the mishmash trees."

Now gombrizils cannot smile, for their faces will not allow them to, but they can laugh, which is what Ut now did.

"Rubbish!" she cried merrily. "You will see all those things."

"But, madam," said the slobbadunk, "I have lost the sight of my eye!"

"No, you haven't," said Ut, "you've just got mud in it. Keep still now and I'll get it out for you," and with her big seventh leg she began, very carefully, to wipe away the mud on the middle of the slobbadunk's forehead. Soon she saw a glint of color, and before long, the one large green eye was clean and clear again.

Tumblerum Wollycobble opened its round rubbery mouth.

"I can see again!" it cried. "I can see you, but how can I ever thank you enough! If ever I can do you a favor, please call upon me, madam."

"Oh, do call me Ut."

"I hardly think I can, madam. You are, after all, a gombrizil, and gombrizils are septipedal."

"What's that mean?" asked Ut.

"Having seven legs," said the slobbadunk. "While I, like all my kind, am an apode."

"What's that mean?"

"No legs. Therefore vastly inferior to an animal such as yourself, madam."

"Oh, but that's nonsense," said Ut. "Legs don't matter, it's brains that count, and you've obviously got lots, knowing such difficult words as those."

The slobbadunk's answer to this was a loud belch.

"I beg your pardon, madam," it said. "I would willingly exchange what brains I have for a decent digestion. When your husband called me 'Windbag' and 'Smellybreath,' I fear that he was speaking the truth."

"It was very rude of him," said Ut, "and I told him so."

"Think nothing of it," said Tumblerum. "As I told you, we Wollycobbles all suffer in the same way, and I myself suffer worst of all." And as if to prove it, he let off a long string of burps.

This noise disturbed a family of filigogs that had been hiding in the slippysloppy grass, and they hopped hastily away, their bushy tails curled over their hairy backs.

Gombrizils are very partial to filigogs, especially tender hairless little ones, and with her sharp-taloned seventh leg, Ut quickly speared three and popped them into her mouth.

"Sorry," she said to the slobbadunk when she had swallowed them, "I should have offered you one."

"No use to me, madam," said Tumblerum. "All slobbadunks are herbivores."

"What's that mean?" asked Ut.

"Vegetarians. We do not eat meat."

"Oh, poor you!" said Ut. "What *do* you eat then?"

"Slippysloppy grass," said the slobbadunk, and it opened its round rubbery mouth and sucked in a great deal of the stuff.

No wonder it gets indigestion, said Ut to herself, *shoveling down all that slimy muck. Herbivore indeed! What it needs is something solid, like one of those filigogs. Or better still,* she thought, *a couple of nice fat swoots,* and being of a softhearted nature, she set off to see if she could find some.

Swoots as a rule live under large flat stones, and Ut, using one or other of her seven legs, turned over a number until she found a colony of swoots: shiny pink, sausage-shaped creatures that wriggled and wiggled in alarm at being suddenly exposed to the light.

Quickly Ut speared and ate all but the two biggest swoots. These she carefully stowed in the useful little pouch that all gombrizils have upon their chests. Then she made her way back to the slobbadunk, guided, of course, by the sound of its ceaseless burping.

"Tumblerum," she said.

"Yes, madam?"

"I can call you Tumblerum, can't I?"

"Of course."

"It's rather a long name. We gombrizils are used to short ones. Could I perhaps call you Tum?"

"Certainly."

"Right," said Ut. "Now listen, Tum. Open your mouth and shut your eye, and I'll give you something as nice as pie."

Obediently, Tumblerum Wollycobble closed its one green eye and opened its round rubbery mouth.

Quick as a flash, Ut reached into her pouch with her seventh leg, speared one of the swoots, popped it between the slobbadunk's rubbery lips, and tickled it under its chin (or where its chin would have been if it had had one) to make it swallow.

Which it did.

Alarmed and horrified at the feeling of the soft, slimy swoot slipping down its throat, the slobbadunk opened its mouth again to protest, whereupon Ut popped in the second swoot.

"There," she said. "Unless I miss my guess, that should do the trick, Tum. No need for you to have gas anymore."

3

Ut went hopping back to the grove of mishmash trees, in whose branches the strollops sat screeching noisily. Beneath the trees, Ut could see Og still looking sulky.

"Og, darling," said Ut quietly, "I'm perfectly serious about something. You are going to come with me and apologize to that slobbadunk to which you were so rude."

"Never!" shouted Og.

Ut took one huge hop that landed her beside her smaller husband.

She raised her seventh leg and two others for good measure, in a manner that was distinctly threatening.

"Og," she said. "You will do as I say. Or else."

Og sighed. *You've got to hand it to the old girl,* he said to himself. *She's the one with nerve. Scared of noth-ing, she is.* He sighed again. *Not like me,* he thought, *frightened of slobbadunks.*

"Come on then," said Ut.

At that moment, they heard a deep voice calling.

"Madam! Madam!" cried the voice, and then they saw, slithering slowly toward them, the

sinuous shape of Tumblerum Wollycobble, the slobbadunk.

"Madam!" it cried again.

"Oh, no!" said Og, and he turned, poised for flight, but Ut stuck the claw of her seventh leg in his pouch, making him a prisoner.

"Now's your chance," she said to him and to the slobbadunk. "Come here, Tum, old boy . . . er, old girl . . . er, old thing. My husband has something to say to you."

"Oh, madam!" said Tumblerum. "It is *I* who have something to say to *you*! Thank you, madam, thank you from the bottom of my heart and the bottom of my stomach and the bottom of my bottom! Listen, please."

They listened for quite a long time, but no further sound came from the slobbadunk's round rubbery mouth.

"What do you hear?" it said at last.

"Nothing," said Ut and Og together.

"Exactly! What would you have expected to hear?"

"Burps!" cried Ut. "Oh, you're not burping anymore! Those swoots did the trick!"

"They did," said Tumblerum. "Thanks to them, I am a martyr to indigestion no longer."

"You're a vegetarian no longer either," said Ut. "Swoots are good red meat, no doubt of that, so you can't call yourself a herbivore anymore."

"I don't care!" cried Tumblerum Wollycobble. "Because of you, my troubles are over. I'm the happiest slobbadunk in the world, and you, madam, are the kindest, cleverest gombrizil, and your husband is the most handsome and, no doubt, the bravest. How sorry I am, sir, that you do not care for slobbadunks. Your lady wife said that you are frightened of us, but that I simply cannot believe. How could a brave gentleman like yourself possibly be scared of a humble creature such as myself?"

Og's three eyes had been out on stalks anyway at the sight of the slobbadunk, but now they began to glisten with pleasure at being called handsome and brave.

"Scared?" he said. "Me? Of you? What an idea!"

"Great!" said Ut. "Well, if you're not scared of my friend Tum, you can stay here with him . . . er, with her . . . er, with it, while I go off and collect a pouchful of swoots. But before I go, let me remind you, Og, that there's one word I haven't yet heard you say to Tum," and she waved her seventh leg somewhat menacingly at her husband.

"What?" said Og.

"Oh," he said.

"Oh, yes," he said, and then, to the slobbadunk, "Sorry for calling you names."

"Think nothing of it, sir," said Tumblerum Wollycobble as Ut hopped off. "Sticks and stones may break my bones (or they would if I had any bones), but words will never hurt me. Still, it's most kind of you to apologize."

A silence fell beneath the mishmash trees, in which the strollops, now full of freeble fruits, slept. A pair of soft-shelled hagafists came out of their burrow and began to graze on the succulent slippysloppy grass.

Tumblerum lay still, waiting for Ut to bring it more swoots.

Og stood stiffly on his seven legs, wondering what to say next to this slobbadunk, which, he found, no longer revolted him. *In fact,* he said to himself, *now I come to think, it's not such a bad sort of beast.*

At last he said, "Nice weather for the time of year, eh? Warm. Dry. No wind."

"No wind!" replied Tumblerum Wollycobble happily. "How right you are, sir!"

At this moment, Ut reappeared, her pouch crammed with wriggling swoots. Quickly she speared one and popped it into the slobbadunk's round rubbery mouth. She felt particularly pleased with life. Her stomach was full, for while swoot hunting, she had caught and eaten a large long-eared spuddick (one of her favorite meals, they were so juicy), and now here was her husband happily conversing with her friend, Tum. Only one thing was needed to make things perfect.

"Og, darling," she said sweetly. "Do you love me?"

Og looked at her. He was pleased with life, too. *How brave I am*, he thought, *I'm not frightened of slobbadunks anymore.*

"Yes, old girl," he said. "I suppose I do."

"And you like Tum and you're going to be friends with him?"

"Yes, old girl," said Og. "I suppose I could."

"Goody, goody!" cried Ut. "Here, have a swoot. Tum won't mind, will you, Tum?"

"Oh, no, madam."

"You'd better have another one yourself."

"If you please, madam. If sir doesn't object?"

"Of course not, Wollycobble, my friend," said Og. "Always remember to do what my wife tells you, and everything will be all right."

"Yes, sir," said the Slobbadunk.

It turned its head to face Ut and she saw its one green eye shut in a big wink.

From then on, the life of Og and Ut under the mishmash trees changed, for Tumblerum Wolly-cobble came to live there, too. Ut, after all, had to catch swoots for it and she didn't want to go looking all over the place to find it, especially as it was now burp-free and so much harder to track down.

Og had made quite a friend of Tum, possibly

because he liked being called handsome and brave and being treated in a most respectful way. He was now more kindly disposed to slob-badunks in general and to this one in particular.

Tumblerum was, of course, in seventh heaven at being treated so nicely by these wonderful gombrizils.

"I cannot thank you enough, madam," it said to Ut, "for all your trouble in catching swoots for me. I only wish there was some favor I might do for you in return."

"There may be, one day, Tum," Ut replied.

In fact, that day was not long in coming.

An interesting fact about gombrizils is that they cannot have babies when they are young, but must wait until they are middle-aged, which Ut now was.

One morning, she came back from swoot hunting to find Og and Tum side by side under the mishmash trees. She emptied her pouch and left them eating happily.

Then she went off into a quiet corner and began to make a nest of mish-mash leaves.

A little later, she came back and said to her husband, "Can you spare a minute, Og?"

"Of course," he replied. "What is it?"

"This," said Ut, and she led him to the nest. There, in the middle, was a large bright blue egg.

"You are to be a father," she said.

"Wonderful!" shouted Og, and he scratched her (gently) with his seventh leg.

"Let's tell Tum!" he said.

When Tumblerum heard the glad news, its one green eye glistened with tears of joy. Most slobbadunks cannot have children, but Tum was so pleased for its new friends.

"Tum," said Ut. "Do you remember saying you'd like to do me a favor one day?"

"Indeed I do, madam."

"Well, you see," said Ut, "I'm going to have a job to keep my egg warm, because of swoot hunting, and I don't suppose Og will sit on it."

"I shan't," said Og.

"You shouldn't, sir," said Tum. "It's no job for such a brave hunter as yourself."

"But," said Ut, "there is one person who could incubate my egg for me, and its name is Tumblerum Wollycobble."

And so, for the next six months (a gombrizil's

egg takes a long time to hatch) Tumblerum lay under the mishmash trees, while safe and warm beneath its huge stomach lay Og and Ut's blue egg.

Partly to help pass the time and partly, it thought, to comfort the baby that was developing inside the egg, the slobbadunk took to singing lullabies in its deep voice. One of them went like this:

How proud and pleased is
Tumblerum,
To have, beneath its ample
tum,
An egg so beautiful and blue.
Oh, lovely egg! I think of you
Throughout each day, throughout each night.
Though you are hidden from my sight
As if I really had been blind,
You're never absent from my mind.
For though I haven't got a leg
To stand on, I've got madam's egg!
Oh, what an honor, what a thrill
To hatch a baby gombrizil!"

All that time Ut worked hard collecting swoots for her babysitter, while Og went hunting for fili-gogs and hagafists and spuddicks for himself.

At last the day came when Tumblerum Wollycobble suddenly felt a movement beneath its huge stomach.

"Madam! Sir!" it cried, and as Ut and Og hurried up, Tum slid slowly sideways, to reveal a lot of broken blue eggshell and a very small, newly hatched gombrizil.

Og and Ut held legs.

"Our baby!" said Ut.

"Is it a boy?" asked Og.

"Don't know," said Ut.

"Sir! Madam! Why not ask it?" said Tum.

So they did.

The baby gombrizil looked at them.

"I'm a girl," she said. "Who are you?"

"I'm Og, your daddy," said Og.

"And I'm Ut, your mommy," said Ut.

The baby looked at Tumblerum Wollycobble.

"What are you?" she said.

"I'm just a humble slobbadunk, miss."

"What's your name?"

"Tum."

"Well," said the baby gombrizil, "you've certainly got a lovely warm tummy, Tum. Thank you very much for hatching me."

"It was a pleasure, miss."

"Can I call you Uncle Tum? Or should it be Auntie Tum?"

"Better just call me Tum, miss."

"But what are we going to call you?" said Og and Ut to their newly hatched daughter. "It has to be short, mind you. All gombrizils have short names."

"Okay," said the baby.

"Excuse me, miss," said Tum, "but do you mean that's what we are to call you?"

"Okay?" said the baby. "Yes. Fine. I'm Okay," and all four of them looked happily at one another under the mishmash trees.

5

Og and Ut were bewitched by their baby daughter. They thought she was quite beautiful and spoiled her rotten. She was, after all, their only child, for a female gombrizil never lays more than one egg in her life, so that each and every baby hatched is an only child.

Ut taught Okay nice manners, and Og taught her to spear things with her little seventh leg, small things like baby swoots. Most of these

Okay ate, but she always stored a few in her tiny pouch to give to Tumblerum Wollycobble, who thought her the most wonderful thing in the world. She was the apple of its eye, and it was happier than it had ever been before.

Once, it thought, *I was a lonely old slobbadunk, friendless and a martyr to indigestion. Now I have two good pals, Kindly Ut and brave, handsome Og, and above all, there is lovely little Okay. I think of her as my own baby. After all, I hatched her.*

As for Okay herself, she was, of course, fond of

her parents, but it was the slobbadunk who was her great friend. *Six months,* she thought, *I spent underneath Tum's warm tummy when I was an egg. How good of it to brood me for so long, I can't thank it enough,* she would say to herself as she carefully withdrew a small succulent swoot from her pouch and popped it into the slobbadunk's round rubbery mouth.

Mostly, Tumblerum was fed—on large swoots—by Ut, though sometimes, on a good hunting day, Og might bring home a soft-shelled hagafist or a filigog or a spuddick, as a present for the slobbadunk. Tum was always touched that Og had thought of it, but it was still a vegetarian at heart. Swoots had to be eaten for its digestion, but Tum liked slippysloppy grass best of all.

Og's presents were never wasted. Ut and Okay polished them off.

Life was good under the mishmash trees.

Until the night of the Great Storm.

Throughout the previous day the weather—which had been hot and dry for some time—had seemed about to change. By evening, the wind had risen and the sky had filled with dark scudding clouds.

As night fell, the three gombrizils and the slobbadunk settled down as usual under the mishmash trees. That is to say, Og and Ut went to sleep side by side in a big nest of leaves, the claw of Ut's seventh leg tucked into Og's pouch in a friendly, comforting kind of way. As for Tumblerum Wollycobble, it slept at the foot of the biggest mishmash tree, and under its huge fat, warm stomach slept Okay. But around about midnight all of them woke with a start at a sudden deafening crash of thunder,

followed by blinding flashes of lightning. A howling wind was flattening the slippysloppy grass, over which the filigogs came hopping wildly. The hagafists and the long-eared spuddicks dashed down their burrows, the strollops flew screeching out of the trees, and only the swoots, under their

large flat stones, were safe from the fury of the storm.

"Hold my leg, Ut, I'm scared!" shouted Og, and he began to cry.

But then, suddenly, there came, right above their heads, a creaking, groaning, tearing noise, as a huge branch of the biggest of the mishmash trees split, broke off, and fell, right on top of Tumblerum Wollycobble, the slobbadunk. It knocked the wind out of its body with a noise that sounded like the loudest of those burps, which it no longer made.

As quickly as it had started, the Great Storm passed, the wind dropped, and the strollops flew back into the treetops.

Ut had only one thought—her precious daughter.

"Okay!" she cried. "Where are you? Are you OK, Okay?" But answer came there none.

"Oh, stop sniveling, Og," said Ut, "and come and help me find her."

Then she saw the fallen branch.

Then she saw what it had fallen on.

"Oh, Tum!" she cried. "Are you all right?" and in answer she heard the slobbadunk's deep tones.

"No, madam," it said. "I can't say I am."

"Are you badly hurt?"

"Bruised, madam, without doubt," said Tum, "but even the biggest branch cannot break my bones."

"Why not?"

"I haven't got any."

"Oh," said Ut. "Oh, good. But oh, where is my little Okay?"

"Yes," said Og, who had stopped crying now that the storm had passed. "Where is she?"

"Underneath me, brave sir," said Tum.

"Well get off her then!"

"I cannot, sir. I am pinned down."

"Oh, Ut!" said Og. "What can we do?"

"Get that branch off Tum, of course," replied Ut.

Both gombrizils reached out with their seventh legs and hooked their claws into the big branch and pulled with all their might, straining backward with their other twelve legs. But they were not strong enough to move it.

"Stay here with Tum," said Ut to Og. "I'm

going for help," and she set off under the mish-mash trees in a series of huge hops.

Generally, gombrizils like to keep themselves to themselves, but they will rally around in a crisis, and before long, Ut brought back nine more gombrizils, three other pairs and a family of father, mother, and a male child. All of them fastened their seventh legs onto the branch.

"When I say 'Pull!'" shouted Og, "we all pull." And he did and they did, and Tumblerum Wolly-cobble managed, somehow, to inflate its big bruised body, and the branch rolled off.

"Quickly, Tum!" screeched Ut. "Get off my little girl!"

With a great effort, the slobbadunk managed to slide itself sideways, and there, all eleven gom-brizils could see, was the figure of Okay, standing on all her seven legs and looking at them with her three eyes.

"Gosh!" she said. "It wasn't half hot under there."

"Oh, darling!" cried Og and Ut together. "Are you all right?"

"I think so," said Okay. "What happened?"

"A big branch fell on Tum," they said.

"Oh, Tum!" cried Okay. "Are you all right?"

The slobbadunk stared fondly at her with its one large green eye in the middle of its forehead, and opened its round rubbery mouth and answered, "Yes, miss."

"Are you hurt?" asked Okay.

"A bit bruised, that's all," said Tum.

It turned its eye upon all the other gombrizils and said in its deep voice, "My thanks to you all, ladies and gentlemen, for rescuing me."

"Yes, thank you!" cried Og and Ut with one voice.

"As long as your daughter's OK," the rescuers said.

"She is, she is, it's her name!" said Og and Ut, and Tum's green eye glistened.

Now the other three pairs of gombrizils made off, and the family of father, mother, and male child were about to follow, when the youngster hopped up to Okay. He was just the same size as she was.

"Is your name really Okay?" he asked.

"Yes."

"Mine's Wow."

"Wow!" said Okay.

"Hope we meet again," he said.

"Me, too."

After the other family had gone, and Okay was

comforting Tum by scratching his fat sides very gently with her seventh leg (which made him rumble softly with pleasure), Ut said to Og, "Nice boy, didn't you think?"

"Huh!" said Og. "Going to marry her before long, I suppose you're thinking!"

"Why not?" said Ut. "I quite fancy being a grandmother one day."

All was quiet now.

The filigogs hopped back, the hagafists and the spuddicks came up out of their burrows, and in the treetops, the strollops cooed contentedly. Under their large flat stones, the swoots cooed contentedly and fatly, waiting, though they knew it not, to become food for the gombrizils and for Tumblerum Wollycobble, the slobbadunk.

"Feeling better, Tum?" Okay asked it.

"Much better, thank you, miss."

"I won't always be a miss," Okay said. "One of these days I'll be a missus."

"Wow!" said Tum.

Okay stretched out her seventh and longest leg, the one that grew beneath her chin, and gently scratched Tumblerum Wollycobble under where its chin would have been if it had had one.

"But you, Tum," she said, "will always be my best friend."

Life under the mishmash trees went on pleasantly. Wow, the boy gombrizil, often came to see Okay and they would play together all day long. It was fun to chase the strollops when they came down to the ground to pick up fallen freeble fruits, but their three favorite games were probably leap-filigog, hop-spuddick and tag-a-hagafist.

Tumblerum Wollycobble, too, was always pleased to see Wow, who never failed to be very nice to it and often brought it little gifts of swoots.

But the problem with life going on pleasantly is that time seems to pass very quickly, and one fine day, many years later, Ut looked at Og and thought how old he had become. *Not that he isn't still the handsomest of gombrizils*, she said to herself, *but he's not as good on his legs as he used to be and his bones are a bit creaky.* At much the same time, Og looked at Ut and said to himself, *Oh, dear, she was such a pretty girl and now, well, she's showing her age and no mistake.*

Okay was by now grown up, as was her boyfriend, Wow, but Og and Ut knew that there was a long time yet to wait before they could hope—if things went right—to become grand-parents.

As for Tumblerum Wollycobble, life went on as usual. Slobbadunks are very, very long-lived and what's more, they continue to look much the same, however old they are. Tum was especially healthy, probably because, unlike the other slobbadunks, it was no longer a martyr to indigestion. Og and Ut still brought it occasional swoots, but they were now too slow to catch much for themselves, and Okay and Wow started to do most of the hunting. Between them, they caught hagafists and spuddicks and filigogs for Og and Ut and brought home, in their pouches, regular rations of swoots for their great friend Tum.

But then one day something happened under the mishmash trees, which made everyone very happy.

Og and Ut were lying side by side in their nest of leaves, gently and affectionately scratching each other with one of their many legs, and idly watching the strollops above feeding on the freeble fruits. Tum was digesting (easily, these days) a huge meal of slippysloppy grass.

Then along came Okay and her boyfriend. Wow marched up to the nest and said to Og, "Could I have a word, sir?"

"Certainly, my boy," replied Og. "What's the trouble?"

"No trouble, sir," said Wow. "At least I hope not. I have come to ask for your daughter's claw in marriage. We wish to wed."

"Please, Daddy!" said Okay. "Can we?"

"Of course, darling!" shouted Ut before her husband could reply.

"Of course, darling," echoed Og, and to Wow he said, "I shall expect you to take the greatest care of my little girl."

As for Tum, its round rubbery mouth opened and out of it came a joyful sound of great excitement and satisfaction, a sound like "Wheeeeeeee!" while the one green eye in the middle of its forehead glistened with tears of happiness.

"Congratulations, sir and madam!" said the slobbadunk, once Okay and Wow had gone off happily together. "Now you can look forward to becoming grandparents."

"We'll have to look a long way forward," said Og. "She's very young."

"Time will pass," said Tum, "and when the happy event does occur, I wonder if I might beg the greatest of favors?"

"What?" said Og.

"May I keep the egg warm, as I did for your daughter?"

"You'll have to ask her," said Og.

"I'm sure she'll say yes, Tum," said Ut. "You did such a good job hatching her."

Okay and Wow made their way out from the shelter of the mishmash trees in a daze of happiness, as the strollops screeched above. Each put a claw into the other's pouch as they hopped along side by side.

"Oh, Wow!" said Okay. "Just think, we're going to be married!"

"If that's OK by you, Okay," Wow replied.

"Oh, Wow! It is! We've always had such fun together!"

And they had, too.

As children, they had spent hours playing games like clawball, where they kicked an unripe freeble fruit about, or different athletic competitions— long jump and high jump (which Wow generally won) and races (in which Okay was usually the winner).

Later, as teenage gombrizils, they hunted together, at first just to get swoots for Tumblerum Wollycobble, but then later, as Og and Ut grew older, the youngsters caught food for them.

The slow, soft-shelled hagafists were easy prey, but the long-eared spuddicks and especially the filigogs that hopped swiftly by, their busy tails curled over their backs, were much more difficult for a single gombrizil to catch. Two gombrizils working together, though, were a different matter and, as Okay was fond of saying, "Wow and I make a great team."

Sometimes they would run the spuddicks and filigogs down, taking turns
in the chase, but mainly they
relied upon ambush.

One of them (Okay,
let's say) would hide
in the deep slippy-
sloppy grass, for ex-
ample, and then Wow
would drive the chosen
creature toward her. Okay would jump out on the
juicy spuddick or fat filigog and catch it easily.

But, of course, they never forgot Tum, and each
day they would collect pouchfuls of the fattest,
most succulent swoots for their friend.

They were talking of Tum as they hopped
along together on this, the day of their engage-
ment.

"It hatched you, didn't it?" Wow said.

"Yes," replied Okay. "The dear thing sat on me for six months, Mommy told me. Who hatched you, Wow, d'you know?"

"My dad," said Wow.

"Not your mom?"

"No. She told him to do it, so he did."

"When I lay an egg," Okay said, "will you sit on it?"

"No way!" said Wow.

"What, you're going to make me sit on it for six months?"

"No," said Wow. "When the time comes, we'll ask old Tum."

As the young gombrizils walked and talked, old Tum was asleep under the mishmash trees. Its large meal of slippysloppy grass was taking quite a bit of digesting, and when it woke, it found that Og and Ut had gone off together, and that it was alone and still rather hungry.

Tum slithered to its larder, a shallow hole between the roots of a big mishmash tree. This store place was the idea of Okay and Wow, and in

it they put supplies of
spare swoots.

Though it was easiest
for Tum to have a swoot
popped into that round
rubbery mouth by one
or other of the young
gombrizils, it could still
manage to feed itself, if left alone, thanks to this
larder. It would peer in with that one green eye in
the middle of its forehead, to make sure that there
were swoots inside (there always were), and then
it would stick its mouth down into the hole and
suck up swoot after swoot.

Now, its hunger satisfied, Tumblerum Wollycobble decided to take a little modest exercise.

In the old days, its progress would have been
marked by an endless series of loud belches, but
now its digestion, thanks to the swoots, was

perfect. Certainly its mouth opened as it slid along but not to emit a burp.

Instead, there came from that round rubbery hole a kind of whistling noise, which sounded rather plaintive but which was, in fact, joyful.

Tum was whistling from pure happiness on that sunny morning as it thought with fondness of the family of gombrizils that had adopted it.

Og, it remembered, had long ago pretended to be frightened—ridiculous for such a brave, handsome creature.

Ut had always been kind to it.

As for Okay, Tumblerum Wollycobble thought of her as a sort of daughter and of Wow, therefore, as a kind of son-in-law.

Then, suddenly, it saw them both, hopping

happily along together. Each of them had their seventh claw in the other one's pouch, for this is how gombrizils hold hands.

"Hullo, Tum!" they cried.

Oh, thought the slobbadunk, *should I ask them if I can hatch their egg now? Or would it be better to wait awhile?* But before it could make up its mind, Okay hopped right up close and stroked its fat back with one of her legs and said, "Tum, dear, we've something to ask you. Will you do us a great favor?"

"Of course, miss, of course, young sir!" said Tum. "What is it?"

"When the time comes for me to lay my egg," said Okay, "will you hatch it, as you did me?"

Tum's one and only green eye glistened with sudden tears.

"Of course, miss!" it cried.

"Great!" they said.

"And please," said Okay, "drop the 'miss' and the 'young sir' and call us by our proper names from now on. You are our special friend, you know."

Slobbadunks cannot smile, due to the shape of their mouths, but Wow and Okay were left in no doubt of their friend's happiness.

"OK, Okay," said Tumblerum Wollycobble joyfully.

The years passed for the happy family under the mishmash trees, and everyone, especially Okay, spent a lot of time wondering when a very special egg would be laid. They wondered when Wow would be a father, when Og and Ut would become the grandparents they longed to be, and when Tum would begin to hatch it.

Each year, Okay grew nearer to middle age, the time when female gombrizils come into lay. Each year, obviously, Og and Ut grew older and more anxious to set eyes on that grandson or granddaughter. They remained in good health, however, despite their age, thanks to a generous diet. Their son-in-law was a mighty hunter, and both the old gombrizils feasted royally on plentiful supplies of tender young hagafists and juicy spuddicks and fine fat filigogs.

"Wow, dear," said Okay one day. "I think I may be coming into lay before too long. I feel ever so full."

"Oh, darling!" cried Wow. "How marvelous! Will it be a boy or a girl, I wonder? What do you think?"

"I'm not sure," replied Okay. "Sometimes I think it's the one and sometimes the other. Better not say anything to Mommy or Daddy yet."

"What about Tum?" asked Wow.

"Well, he doesn't need to know until the egg is laid."

Which it was, not many days later.

Okay and Wow had their own bed of leaves under the mishmash trees, some little distance from Og and Ut's, and early one morning, Wow was woken by Okay saying, "Go and get some swoots for Tum, there's a good boy."

"What, this early?" yawned Wow. "Can't it wait a bit?"

"No, it can't!" said Okay in an angry voice. "Now push off, do."

"Females," said Wow to himself as he staggered off into the dawn. "There's no understanding them."

But he understood well enough when he came back with a pouchful of swoots, for there was his wife standing proudly over the nest, while beneath her, in between her seven long legs, was a big beautiful, bright blue egg!

"Oh, dearest!" cried Wow. "You've done it! Are you all right! How do you feel?"

"To tell the truth," replied Okay, "I still feel full."

She shifted uncomfortably.

"What can you mean?" asked Wow, as his wife settled down again upon the nest.

"Look the other way!" said Okay sharply.

Obediently, Wow did as he was bidden. Then he heard a kind of grunt and then a sort of plop.

"You can turn around now," said Okay, and when Wow did so, she stood up again and there in the nest were two eggs, side by side. One was blue, the other was pink.

Wow was speechless. Gombrizils only ever have one child, his mother had told him, yet now it seemed he was the father of . . . twins!!

"Go and fetch Tum," said Okay.

When the slobbadunk eventually arrived, Okay stepped from the nest.

"What do you see, Tum?" she asked.

Tumblerum Wollycobble's one green eye nearly popped out of its head.

"Two, miss! I mean, two, Okay!" it gasped. "However . . . ? I mean, your mother and father told me that gombrizils never lay more than one egg."

"Well," said Okay, "Mommy and Daddy were

wrong, it seems. We were all wrong. But are you willing to sit on both of them?"

"Of course, Okay," said Tum. "It makes no difference to me. I'll be on duty for six months anyway."

"Dear, kind, Tum," said Okay. "But promise me you won't say anything to my mom and dad. They'll think you're sitting on one egg, and if anything goes wrong, I mean, if only one should hatch out, they'll never know."

"Nothing is going to go wrong," said Tum firmly. "Shall I start now?"

"Yes, please," said Okay.

"Jolly good show, Tum," said Wow.

The slobbadunk looked thoughtfully at the two gombrizil eggs in the nest.

"Different colors," it said. "Do you think that perhaps . . . ?"

"Yes!" said Okay, "with a bit of luck. Blue for a

girl, we know—the egg you hatched me from was blue—and pink for a boy."

And would you believe it, that's how things turned out.

Six months dragged by, maddeningly slowly for the proud parents and the expectant grandparents, while Tumblerum Wollycobble sat stolidly upon the nest, well fed by Okay and Wow on swoots and on supplies of slippysloppy grass that they scratched up with their sharp claws.

The strollops perched above, dropping occasional ripe freeble fruits, which were fed to Tum, and waiting to carry news of the birth to every other gombrizil and slobbadunk, hagafist, spuddick, and filigog. When it happened, only the swoots, lying fatly under their big flat stones, would not know straightaway.

As he had while brooding Okay, Tum sang to the two eggs beneath him:

"Oh, what a bit of luck! Just think,
There's two of you, one blue, one pink,
We'll simply have to wait and see
What sort of gombrizils you'll be.
I wonder, will you both be hes?
Or will the pair of you be shes?
Or will it be one girl, one boy,
To give your mom and dad such joy,
One like Okay and one like Wow?

There isn't any knowing how
It all will end when out you come
From underneath your loving Tum.

For the rest of their lives Og and Ut would never forget the hatching day.

They were woken early by Wow calling, "Quick! Come quick!" and they hopped slowly and sleepily after him.

"Oh, Og!" said Ut. "I hope it's a boy, brave and handsome like you."

"Oh, Ut!" said Og. "I hope it's a girl, quick and clever as you are."

They came to the nest where Okay was waiting and where Tum still lay, its bulk concealing whatever was there. Then the slobbadunk slowly slithered out of the mess of brushed leaves and broken eggshell, some blue, some pink, to reveal not one, but two tiny gombrizils.

"Say hello to Grandpa and Grandma," said Okay, and the babies squeaked.

"Two!" said Og in utter amazement.

"What are they?" said Ut.

"Gombrizils," replied Og.

"No, no," said Ut. "I mean—are they girls or boys or what?"

"Ask them, Mommy," said Okay.

Ut bent down over the nest.

"Listen, children," she said softly, and she pointed to one of the twins.

"What are you?" she asked.

"I'm a girl," the baby replied.

Ut pointed to the other, which had a little bit of pink shell still stuck on its back.

"And you?"

"I'm a boy," said the other baby.

"Many congratulations, Wow, my lad," said Og to his son-in-law.

"Okay, darling," said Ut to her daughter. "No gombrizil has ever done such a thing before!"

"I only laid the eggs, Mommy," said Okay. "It was Tum who hatched them."

"A privilege," said Tumblerum Wollycobble in his deep voice, while above their heads the strollops, eager to spread the amazing news, flew screeching out of the mishmash trees.

*   *   *

What a happy family it was that now lived under those trees!

After much discussion, Okay and Wow had settled upon names for the newly hatched twins, names which must, of course, be pretty short ones. The girl was to be called Bluebell, the boy Pinky, and each was already hopping happily about on its seven little legs.

It was not long before that memorable day when the twins first brought presents for their grandparents.

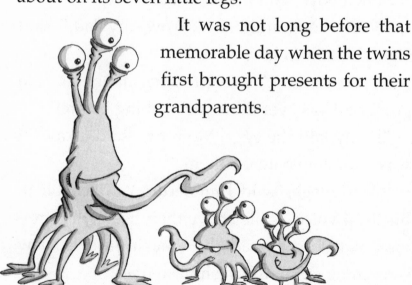

Bluebell pulled out from her little pouch a tiny, soft-shelled hagafist and Pinky had speared a small swoot.

"Oh, you clever darlings!" cried Ut. "You're going to be great hunters like your daddy!"

"And your grandpa," said Og with his mouth full of hagafist.

Ut picked up Pinky's swoot and hopped slowly over to a particular leafy hollow under a particular mishmash tree, which was where Tumblerum Wollycobble, the slobbadunk, could usually be found.

It looked up as she approached, staring fondly at her out of that one large green eye.

"Like a swoot, Tum?" she asked.

"Oh, thank you, madam," said the slobbadunk. "You are so good to me."

"Well, you're one of the family," Ut said. "You

hatched Okay for me and you hatched Bluebell and Pinky for Okay."

Even as she spoke, the twins appeared.

"Morning, Uncle Tum," said Bluebell, and "Morning, Auntie Tum," said Pinky, and off they hopped.

The slobbadunk watched them for a moment

and then it turned to Ut and opened that round rubbery mouth.

"Oh, madam, dear madam," it said. "To think of all that you have done for me since first we met. You helped me when I thought I had gone blind; you cured my indigestion; you saved me on the day of the Great Storm. How can I ever thank you enough?"

"No need, Tum," said Ut. "It is I who have to thank you. You mean so much to my grand-children, to my daughter, to my son-in-law, to my husband, and most of all, to me. You are my best friend."

A large tear ran out of Tum's green eye. Its round rubbery mouth opened but no words came out, only a deep sigh of contentment.

In happy silence, Ut, the gombrizil, and Tum-blerum Wollycobble, the slobbadunk, enjoyed each other's company, under the mishmash trees.